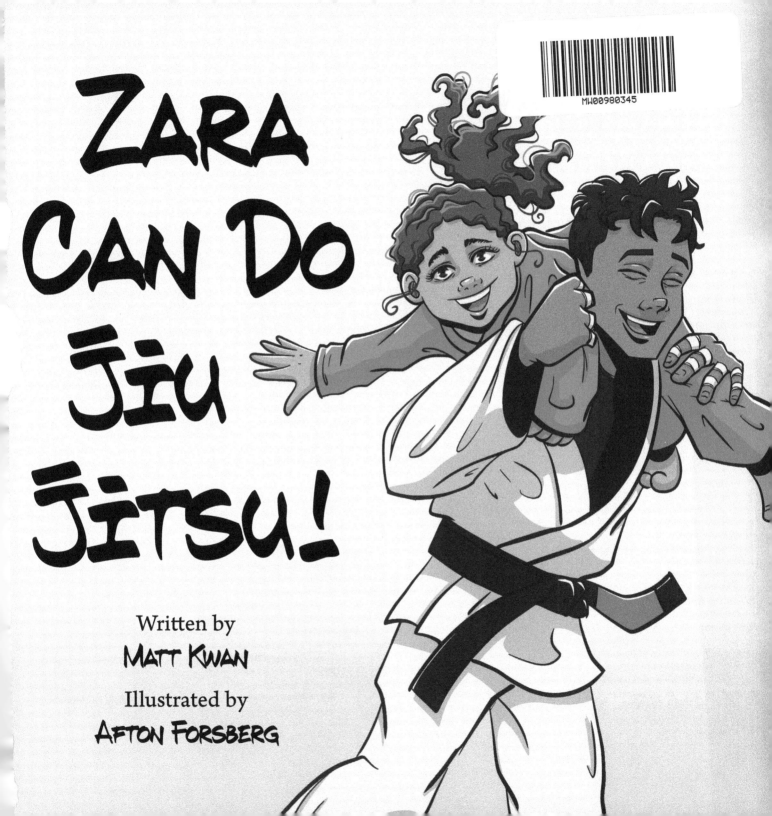

Zara Can Do Jiu Jitsu!

Written by
Matt Kwan

Illustrated by
Afton Forsberg

"ZARA, are you ready to train?
The time for JIU JITSU is here again!"

"Let's pack our stuff
and put on our shoes.
My GI is white,
which colour do you choose?"

I choose my favourite colour, blue,
my **WHITE BELT** has a black bar too.
My friends are waiting at the gym,
for **Jiu Jitsu** class to begin!

Daddy's belt is **BIG** and **BLACK**,
and has a **RED BAR** attached.
Without looking down
his belt he's tying,
he ties his belt without even trying!

The kids quickly line up, we're quiet now;
the time has come for us to **BOW**.
Our belts are tied and **GIS** are checked,
we all bow in to show **RESPECT**.

We tuck and tumble, leap and **ROLL**.
Daddy says to use **CONTROL**.
Some kids can do it and some can not,
but doing my best helps a lot.

We train to safely fall and then,
we pick ourselves back up again.
We fall and fall and fall some more,
and learn to safely hit the floor.

After practicing our falls and flips,
we hit the ground and move our hips.
The **SHRIMP** is what we call this move,
we hip **ESCAPE** and make it smooth.

We slap and bump; it's time to roll!
We try to GRIP lapels and folds.
We all stay SAFE while playing rough,
this sport is fun and makes you TOUGH!

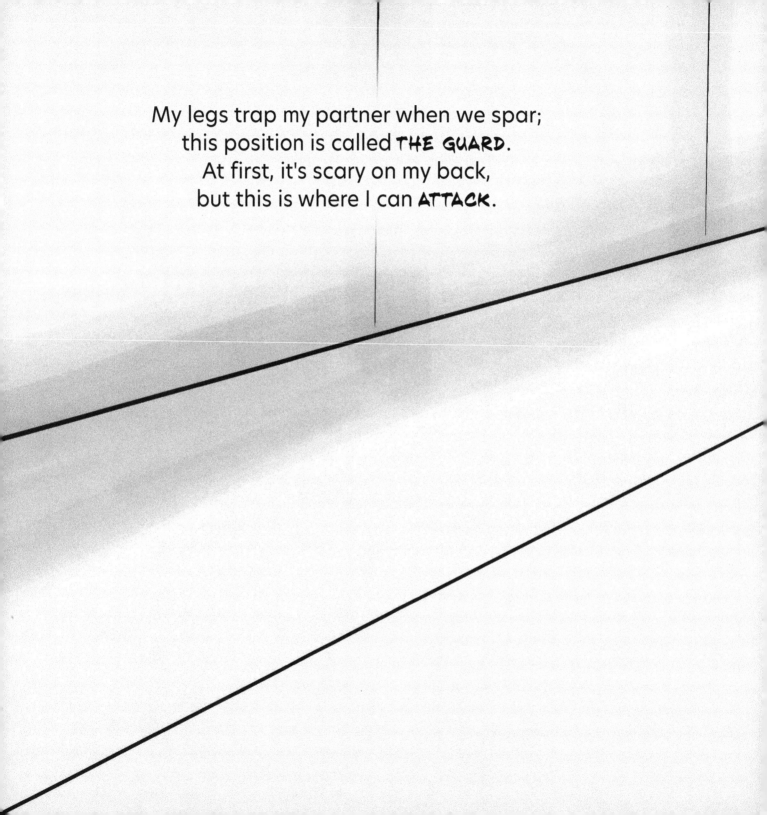

My legs trap my partner when we spar;
this position is called **THE GUARD**.
At first, it's scary on my back,
but this is where I can **ATTACK**.

The **ARMBAR** is my favourite thing.
Daddy calls me the armbar king!
My partner's arm is fully trapped,
I bridge my hips to get the **TAP**.

I'm trapped inside my partner's lap,
sometimes it's me who has to TAP.
It doesn't hurt to lose to friends,
we slap and bump and ROLL again.

Sometimes other kids start crying,
but they shake it off and keep on trying.
Fall down seven times and get up eight,
we **FACE OUR FEARS** and it feels great!

The end of class has come already.
We feel tired and pretty sweaty.
We make a line and stand with care.
We fix our gis, our belt, and hair.

On the way home, in the car,
Daddy says he watched me spar.
He sees the things that I can do,
and the things I can IMPROVE.
He makes it clear he's proud of me
for training Jiu Jitsu so bravely.

"I want to be like you," I say.
"Will I ever be a black belt one day?"
Daddy smiles and says, "I know you will,
in every class you learn a new **SKILL**.
Here's the thing about goals far away-
if you **WORK HARD**, they'll be yours one day."

Glossary

ARMBAR: This is a classic joint lock in Jiu Jitsu. The armbar has the potential to break your opponent's arm by hyperextending at the elbow joint.

BRAZILIAN JIU JITSU: A grappling martial art that revolves around ground work and submission holds. Jiu Jitsu translates to "The gentle art." Jiu Jitsu matches begin from the standing position.

BLACK BELT: One of the highest ranks in Brazilian Jiu Jitsu.

BREAKFALL: This is how grapplers practice falling safely. The impact from the fall transfers from the torso to the limbs by timing the fall and slapping the floor.

CHOKE: A submission that can result in unconsciousness, due to the closure of your opponent's carotid arteries.

CLINCH: A standing position in grappling where both athletes have grips on each other.

DOJO: The gym or training room where Martial Arts are practiced.

ESCAPE: A movement used to exit a disadvantageous position.

FRAMES: Using a portion of your body as a structure to manage the distance between yourself and your opponent.

GI: The traditional Jiu Jitsu uniform; Kimono. In Jiu Jitsu and Judo, the gi can be gripped and manipulated to gain control over your opponent, utilize throws, amplify pinning pressure, and apply finishing holds.

GRAPPLING: Any fighting sport that can involve takedowns, ground work, and submission holds. Grappling sports do not involve striking.

GUARD: This position is what sets Brazilian Jiu Jitsu apart from all other martial arts. The guard is classified as any bottom position where your legs manage distance between you and your opponent.

GUARD PASS: One of the main objectives from the top position is to "pass the guard", which means moving past your partner's legs. This allows for more advantageous finishing positions in grappling and in fighting.

HOOKS: Using your feet to grip your partner's limbs or torso.

JUDO: An Olympic sport that is based around throwing your partner flat on their shoulders. There are submissions and ground work as well, but the majority of the sport takes place from the standing position. Judo translates to "The gently way".

KIMURA: A figure-4 joint lock that targets the shoulder joint of your opponent. The technique involves using both of your arms to rotate your opponent's arm behind their back. The move is named after Japanese Judo legend Masahiko Kimura.

LAPEL: The portion of the gi jacket immediately below (and is an extension of) the collar.

MOUNT: A dominant position in grappling where one athlete straddles the other athlete's torso on both knees. This is a devastating position to attack from in grappling and in fighting.

OSS: In Brazilian Jiu Jitsu, this term is used to acknowledge an instruction or difficult task, to show respect, or as a greeting.

PULL GUARD: This movement is used from the standing position, where one athlete transitions to the guard (by sitting down or jumping) in order to avoid being taken down.

REAR MOUNT: A dominant position in grappling, where one athlete is behind the other, with both arms and legs wrapped around their opponent. This is often considered the best position in the sport to employ submissions from.

RED BELT: The highest rank attainable in Brazilian Jiu Jitsu. You must be at least 67 years old to achieve the Red Belt rank.

RE-GUARD: To recover your guard from a disadvantageous position.

ROLL/ROLLING: To execute a roll, or the universal Brazilian Jiu Jitsu term to describe sparring.

SHRIMP: A fundamental defensive movement in Jiu Jitsu where the practitioner moves their hips to create space, with the intention of regaining their guard.

SLAP AND BUMP: The universal Brazilian Jiu Jitsu handshake.

SPAR: To fight in the training room. To practice with live resistance.

STRIPE: Stripes on a practitioner's belt that represents the skill/degrees between belts.

SUBMISSION: A finishing hold with the potential to end the fight by way of strangulation or damage to a targeted joint.

SWEEP: A technique which transitions one athlete from the bottom guard position to the top position.

TAKEDOWN: When one athlete takes the other athlete to the ground from the standing position with control.

TAP/TAPPING OUT: This is how you give up or "submit" in Jiu Jitsu. The goal of the sport is to make your partner give up, usually by some form of strangulation or joint lock.

THROW: A move used from the standing position, where one athlete takes the other athlete down.

TORI: The person doing the technique.

TRIANGLE: An iconic submission in Jiu Jitsu, where one athlete strangles the other athlete with their own arm, using their legs in a closed figure-4 configuration.

UKE: Training partner; the person receiving the technique.

 FriesenPress

One Printers Way
Altona, MB R0G 0B0
Canada

www.friesenpress.com

ISBN
978-1-03-915713-2 (Hardcover)
978-1-03-915712-5 (Paperback)
978-1-03-915714-9 (eBook)

1. JUVENILE FICTION, SPORTS & RECREATION, MARTIAL ARTS

Distributed to the trade by The Ingram Book Company

CPSIA information can be obtained
at www.ICGtesting.com
Printed in the USA
BVHW012021250123
656779BV00002B/3